Ourselves

*For all our years*
*on the farm*

❧

First published 2002
by Walker Books Ltd
87 Vauxhall Walk
London SE11 5HJ

2 4 6 8 10 9 7 5 3 1

© 2002 Kim Lewis

This book has been typeset in Galahad Mixed

Printed in Italy

British Library Cataloguing in Publication Data:
a catalogue record for this book is available
from the British Library

ISBN 0-7445-8842-1

# A Quilt for Baby

Kim Lewis

WALKER BOOKS
AND SUBSIDIARIES

LONDON · BOSTON · SYDNEY

Mother was making
a quilt for Baby,
stitching it with care.
As she sewed each
patchwork square,
Mother softly talked
to Baby. She told the
story of the quilt.
And this is what she said.

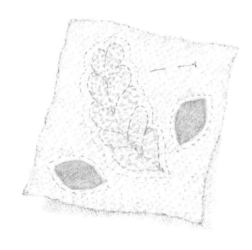

"There is a farm far away from the town in a valley in the hills where a river runs. Here the skies are high and wide. The wind makes trees grow crooked. Dry stone walls edge all the fields and animals graze in the meadows. There's an old stone farmhouse with barns near by. This is home, my little one. This is where we live.

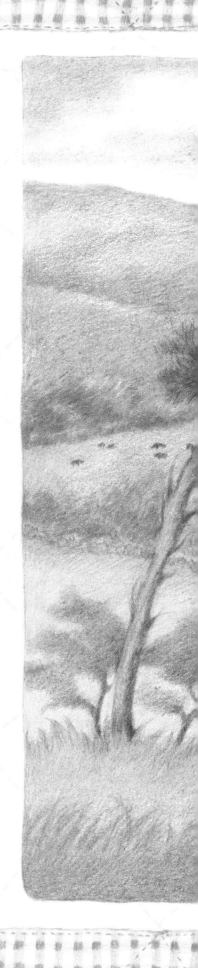

"Up on the hills below the
high wide skies are our
sheep and lambs.
'Are you there?' calls a ewe
to her little lamb.
'I am,' says the lamb, 'I am.'
Close by there's a ram with
curling horns. He is the little
lamb's father.

"And in the fields above the valley, Floss, our collie, gathers sheep with your daddy. All day long they work. Floss's little puppy, Sam, wants to help. 'One day you will,' says Floss to Sam.

"Down by the river in the summer sun our cows are happily grazing. A little calf skips around his mother. 'Watch me run,' says the little calf.

Our big red bull just stands and stares. 'What's the hurry, little calf?' he says.

"In a field edged round by dry stone walls our mare runs through the grass. Her little foal frisks along beside her. 'Can you smell the fresh new grass?' neighs the mare. 'I can, I can,' neighs her little foal.

"In a meadow with a crooked tree our cockerel puffs and crows. Hens come running for their food. They scratch and peck and poke. Their little chicks are always cheeping.

'Peep, peep, peep, peep, peep!' they go.

"And here is our goose,
who flaps her wings as
washing blows on the line.
'I love windy days!' honks
the goose.
'Will I have wings like that?'
her little gosling wonders.

"Snug in a byre there's our nanny goat with her two little newborn kids. Bill and Joe are twins, so it's hard to tell which one is which.

Is that Bill butting his mother gently? Is that Joe nuzzling for his mother's milk?

"And in the barn beside our farmhouse, Tom the cat is prowling. Our mother cat curls up warm in the hay as night-time comes to the hills and the valley.
'Are you sleepy?' purrs the mother cat. But her little kitten is fast asleep."

And when the quilt was finished, Mother wrapped it round her baby. She kissed Baby as she softly said, "This is a quilt for you, to comfort you and keep you warm. Here are pictures of our farm in the valley. Here are our sheep below high wide skies and our collies working on the hills. Here are our cows and horses and hens, and our geese blown by the wind. Here are the barns and here is our farmhouse. Here are our goats and cats.

"Now sleep, Baby, sleep,
for you are here with
me and Daddy.
And before too long
we'll walk with you
on the hills above our farm.
For this is home,
my little one.
This is where we live."

For all our years
on the farm

ও

First published 2002
by Walker Books Ltd
87 Vauxhall Walk
London SE11 5HJ

2 4 6 8 10 9 7 5 3 1

This book has been typeset in Galahad Mixed

Printed in Italy

British Library Cataloguing in Publication Data:
a catalogue record for this book is available
from the British Library

ISBN 0-7445-8842-1

# A Quilt for Baby

## Kim Lewis

WALKER BOOKS

AND SUBSIDIARIES

LONDON · BOSTON · SYDNEY

Mother was making
a quilt for Baby,
stitching it with care.
As she sewed each
patchwork square,
Mother softly talked
to Baby. She told the
story of the quilt.
And this is what she said.

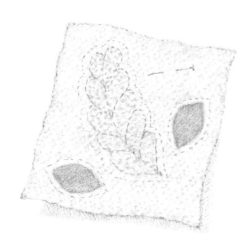

"There is a farm far away from the town in a valley in the hills where a river runs. Here the skies are high and wide. The wind makes trees grow crooked. Dry stone walls edge all the fields and animals graze in the meadows. There's an old stone farmhouse with barns near by. This is home, my little one. This is where we live.

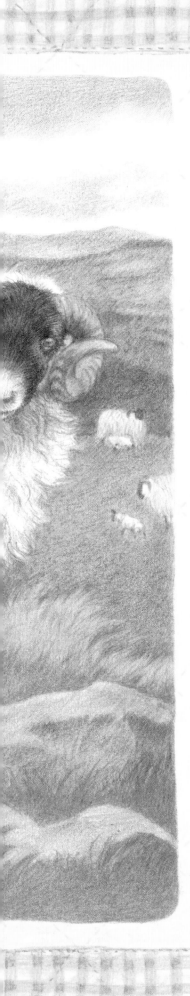

"Up on the hills below the high wide skies are our sheep and lambs.

'Are you there?' calls a ewe to her little lamb.

'I am,' says the lamb, 'I am.' Close by there's a ram with curling horns. He is the little lamb's father.

"And in the fields above the valley, Floss, our collie, gathers sheep with your daddy.
All day long they work. Floss's little puppy, Sam, wants to help.
'One day you will,' says Floss to Sam.

"Down by the river in the summer sun our cows are happily grazing. A little calf skips around his mother. 'Watch me run,' says the little calf.

Our big red bull just stands and stares. 'What's the hurry, little calf?' he says.

"In a field edged round by dry stone walls our mare runs through the grass. Her little foal frisks along beside her. 'Can you smell the fresh new grass?' neighs the mare. 'I can, I can,' neighs her little foal.

"In a meadow with a crooked tree our cockerel puffs and crows. Hens come running for their food. They scratch and peck and poke. Their little chicks are always cheeping.

'Peep, peep, peep, peep, peep!' they go.

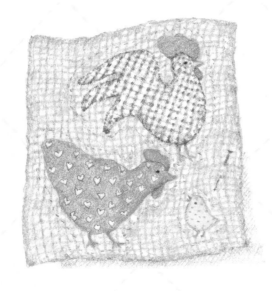

"And here is our goose,
who flaps her wings as
washing blows on the line.
'I love windy days!' honks
the goose.
'Will I have wings like that?'
her little gosling wonders.

"Snug in a byre there's our nanny goat with her two little newborn kids. Bill and Joe are twins, so it's hard to tell which one is which.

Is that Bill butting his mother gently? Is that Joe nuzzling for his mother's milk?

"And in the barn beside our farmhouse, Tom the cat is prowling. Our mother cat curls up warm in the hay as night-time comes to the hills and the valley.
'Are you sleepy?' purrs the mother cat. But her little kitten is fast asleep."

And when the quilt was finished, Mother wrapped it round her baby. She kissed Baby as she softly said, "This is a quilt for you, to comfort you and keep you warm. Here are pictures of our farm in the valley. Here are our sheep below high wide skies and our collies working on the hills. Here are our cows and horses and hens, and our geese blown by the wind. Here are the barns and here is our farmhouse. Here are our goats and cats.

"Now sleep, Baby, sleep,
for you are here with
me and Daddy.
And before too long
we'll walk with you
on the hills above our farm.
For this is home,
my little one.
This is where we live."